Speculize

Susannah Heffernan

ActivistLit

For Katy

Contents

Preface vii

Seahorses 1

Take No Prisoners 11

The Greys 19

New Marshalsea 21

I don't have an answer for that. Is there something else
    I can help with? 29

The Eyes 33

The Bottle Vault 35

Acknowledgements 41

About the Author 43

Preface

It's often argued that dystopian fiction says more about the way society is than realistic fiction ever can. It's a medium for looking at how we live, and highlighting the dangers and reinforcing the values we hold precious as we look to a future where anything could happen. It's an opportunity to speculate and analyse. Hence the title of this collection: *Speculize*.

In the following pages, I offer you short tales, flash fiction, a poem, and a couple of vignettes. These are intended as brief glimpses into the possible worlds ahead of us. I will be very glad if they give you pause for thought. Make of them what you will.

When I was writing all these pieces, I was world-building. At the time of publication, London, the UK, in fact the great majority of the world is under lockdown because of the Covid19 pandemic, and consequently it has shockingly and suddenly changed the ways we go about our day-to-day life. When we emerge from this period of 'social distancing' things will be different: some things for worse, some for better. Because of this, it felt like the right time for these stories.

Susannah Heffernan, May 2020

Seahorses

Matthias Devachan's no angel, despite his name: he's a Degenerate and an In-valid. But he believes that true heaven's a place on Earth, and in heaven, love comes first. At least, he heard that once, in a song, but it was a long time ago. Too long ago to really remember.

He's walking toward the ticket barriers at Canary Wharf station on a cold Spring morning. The sun is leaking in, streaming down, bright white and glinting off the dilapidated steel escalators as he descends to the Underground platform. He feels the sun on his back like a kind hand, receding. Gorgeous models on huge plasma advertising boards look down upon him like golden goddesses. He returns their gaze, defiant. He's *excellent*, he reminds himself. Train doors part and the Ables push him aside; it's their right, but he toes a couple of them quietly in the shins and smiles, slipping into the carriage, leaning his back against the glass partition which divides him from them, and getting on with his morning pranayama.

He breathes in for four counts. He's got used to doing this behind his muffler. They can't see his face. A small thing, but it makes him feel powerful. The fabric warms his skin. It's made of saffronskene, from New China. Antiviral. He holds his breath for four, breathes out for four. Well worth the investment of a month's benefits to protect his precious vocal cords. He fingers his seahorse necklace, glaring back at a prematurely ageing woman who's staring at his scarf, red-eyed, mouth turned down. Leathery skin sags around her jowls. 'Drain on society,' she trills, turning to the absent-looking faces next to her. Matthias chides himself. No good, those negative thoughts; and he turns his attention inward, feeling his belly rise and fall, setting his intention for the day. To *create*. Create something. And to stay alive. He's learned to ignore these overt taunts. If he reacts, they'll cart him off to the Hospital. It doesn't take much to provoke them. He tunes himself back into his practice, his beta waves flowing, his pulse slowing now.

Matthias considers his options for this morning. He could go and do a full session of yoga, or he could visit his studio and write a song. He could sit on this train and go round and round on the Tube all damn day, and no-one could touch him for that. It's not a crime, as such. He's fortunate, in a blackly comic sort of way, he reminds himself, to have been designated an In-valid, while the Ables, the supposedly fit, get no remission from long working hours, day in, day out. Ridiculous. Unjust. He should feel sorry for them. But he can't quite bring himself to do that. The train judders to a halt.

Once off the carriage, Matthias shows his open palms to the station bot. He offers his necklace too, and the machine runs the usual scan to see if he's tried taking it off. Of course, he hasn't. There's no point. He breathes deeply again, and the beta wave read-out shows he's not agitated. He smiles as he pulls down his muffler to show his face. He's got nothing to hide. He's written only a few compositions this whole year, and he's made no attempts to sing in public, so there's nothing incriminating on his record since his last check-up. The exit barriers hiss as they slide apart. It's even colder here, so he pulls his coat to and zips himself up. His studio door's a few steps along a pedestrianised square. He looks up to check the configurations of today's chemtrails. They look more or less the same as yesterday's: sharp, white intersections, nothing fluffy, the slate-grey sky behind, and he reminds himself that straight lines don't really exist in nature. He closes his eyes and visualises spirals. Spirals of life, spinning. Spinning in the sky, spinning in his chest. Spinning all along his spine. And for a moment, he feels he can rise above it: this world of utilitarians. He presses his muffler tighter around his jaw and edges it up to cover the whole of his nose.

He walks past the bright videowalls to his little music studio, which is nestling between the In-valid yoga space and the In-valid refuge for those with genetic book addiction. He beeps the door with a nod, catching a sneering look from an Able passing by: a suited youngun, fast-stepping towards the great glass entrance of Ernst and Young at the end of the street to spend his day profitably, not aimlessly. Matthias's eyes follow him as he crosses the square, following the lean elegance of his thighs and his firm glutes.

Once inside, Matthias pads along the hall, dodging a couple of old bikes. He sits down heavily on a tatty sofa by the kitchen. Petrus sees him and smiles. 'I didn't think you were coming today, my man,' he says. They sit together for a couple of minutes, saying nothing, listening to guitars and keyboards riffing in the next room, the odd discordant note, and a few pauses and repetitions. Matthias takes off his muffler, but it's still too cold.

3

'You know, Petrus, I was thinking. We're not getting any younger.' Matthias loses the swagger and the attitude he wears when he's outside. In here, he can let them fall. In here, he can be. Not just appear to be. But he can't live his whole life in here and shut the world out, much as the world wants to shut him away. The defences come down now as the repeated bars of a tune half-formed drift in and around him, and he can't help but put a few words to it in his head. He hums along and closes his eyes as it comes to him, in phrases, the beginnings of a vocal melody, plaintive, in a minor key. He looks at the walls covered in art. No word for that outside of here, nothing in the digitised adverts, the bot-composed tunes-on-demand that enable the mainstream day-to-day. No time to think too much about it, they say. They like it. More of the same. They love it. Anything different is a threat. There are no longer any threats in their world.

Petrus puts his big arms around him. His friend's breath is warm and slightly sweet, and Petrus takes Matthias's hands in a strong grip. He kisses him on the forehead. The years have run on but still Petrus is able to soothe him. So many times, Matthias and Petrus have sat like this. Petrus has always held him. Held onto him like this, and he could so easily let Petrus go on holding him, give Petrus what he wants, and give himself some peace, but it's not enough. That's Matthias's problem: nothing's ever enough.

'Have some mango. I think it's ready.' Petrus gets up and goes around the big old wooden table where he's been cooking and reaches into the transparent box where plump fruit and veg are growing in the intense electric beam of a solarbrite. 'Think yourself lucky we don't have to survive on the plastic shit like they do. Look how fresh this is'. He pours him a hot tumbler of gin and comes back. Matthias grips Petrus' wrist, nods, and breathes in the aromatics, bringing the little glass to his nostrils, and he tastes the sweet fruit.

'You're right, I know, but I just wonder how much longer we can go on like this. I mean, there are so few of us now. And I can't stand it that whatever we write, no one will ever hear it. I ...'

Petrus looks at him, his mouth drawn down in a straight line, and neither speaks now. The clamouring noise of a siren screams nearby. Matthias's heart bolts in his chest. It's ultra-high pitched, and like a blade, it thrusts at his head; it's designed to fry the synapses. The vibrations thud and wail as the ambulance parks right outside. They've scurried like rodents to look out of the window.

It's the refuge. They've come for someone in the refuge. There are voices. Arguing. A tin door slamming. *Don't come. They want a reaction. Stay indoors. Wait. Be safe.* The message on Matthias's beep is fleeting but clear. He screws his hand into a fist and pushes his knuckles at the wall. Pushes, and grinds his teeth. 'It's Georgias!' Petrus cries. The ambulance has got him. The noise stops. The vehicle drives away in silence.

'He took his book outside.'

'When?'

'Yesterday. I knew this would happen. It's like he knew it too. It's like he wanted it.' Petrus walks back to the sofa and sits. Resigned. His forearms and hands are shaking.

Matthias grabs a pencil off the shelf next to him and runs it back and forth between his fingers. His head is too full. He's silent. They're both silent. There's hectic chatter in the room where the music was. He throws the pencil at the floor and apologises.

'I'll sort my head out,' he says, eventually. He reaches across to take more mango from his friend. 'I need to get away. I could visit the Lido. They can't stop us.'

'No, they can't, that's true.' Petrus rubs his jaw. 'Just be careful.'

***

The grey frontage of the leisure complex is a copy of Philippe Starck. It's shaped like a shell. Matthias watches the Able scatter like tiny crabs from underneath it. The bullet train has shot him from London to New Amsterdam in twenty minutes via the Causeway. He is in the east of the city and his refuge is a dilapidated hotel from the 1980s. The Grand. It's fenced off for his type. It's a relief from the reflective panelling and the shiny frontages of the high street, which are not for him; its dirty walls and broken windows welcome him. He checks himself in and beeps his dinner order. His top-floor room is tiny and made to feel even smaller by the thrown-together furniture, a real-leather chair and a narrow wooden bed. It's meant to make him feel uncomfortable, but he likes the organic feel. This will be his world for the next two weeks. He stands by the bed, looks at the shelf of real paper books, and thinks of Georgias. He takes one at random and stares out of the window. He just caresses the pages in his hands. The top of the building overlooks the Lido, a man-made beach where the Able come for a couple of days once a year for their scheduled holiday by the artificial water. The real beaches, of course, can't be wasted on tourism. He, as an idler, can come any time he likes, as long as he stays out of the way. They sprawl on the sand, fully clothed in the dull outdoors, not caring to imagine the long-concealed sun behind the grey, and they listen to regimented music from their cochlear chips, or let their audiobooks speak facts to them, and look at animations of laughing holidaymakers projected on the walls of the little compound for them to copy. A few of them have stripped to their wetsuits and are swimming in the pool. No-one is aimlessly playing. Everything has purpose. They've paid good money, from honest work. They're having the time of their lives.

Then Matthias sees him. Such a beautiful young man. His hair is honey-blond, and he has broad shoulders for his age. His back curves elegantly to smooth, taught haunches and his legs are hanging restless over the side of a metal deck chair. How old is he? Twenty? He's sitting on his own behind a tree, and he's got something in his hand. Matthias can see everything from his vantage point. What's he doing? Matthias looks more closely; he can't be sure. He gasps. The man is drawing.

He can't be. Not there. He isn't wearing a necklace. He's an Able. Matthias checks. He leans forward. And he watches as the Able gets up, places his drawing under a towel and walks around the tree to where his group of friends lie, all listening to their headchips. A girl slaps his leg and shouts. Thaddeus! His name? He wriggles his ankle free of her grasp and dives down next to her, wrestling in the sand with her for a moment, quite correctly. He lies still with her head on his chest, and she curls up close to him. He pulls a blanket over them both and they fall asleep. Matthias keeps watching them. He wants to go and look at the young man's drawing. He is at once puzzled and excited. He grabs and holds his seahorse necklace, totem of his precious, abnormal hippocampus; his shameful diagnosis. He's conscious of the fast, hard beating of his heart beneath his hand.

'How's the hotel?' Petrus' easy voice is in his ear.

'Hi, amigo. All good. Scruffy chic, you know, the way I like it. All I need now is an old motorbike.'

'You old romantic.' Petrus' laughter fades away, and Matthias smiles. He starts to read the page of the small volume he took from the shelf:

I saw the best minds of my generation destroyed by madness …

He fingers the yellowy pages at the corners as he imbibes the words.

… angel-headed hipsters burning for the ancient heavenly connection …

Matthias feels his breath quicken. He looks out over the fake beach where the light is dimming. The spot-lit swimming pool looks almost pretty now. He stands up and leans on the sill. He presses his face to the glass, heaves up the old sash and sticks his head out. He gulps in the air.

Matthias runs downstairs. He enters the compound. The sand is soft and fine. Despite the chill air, Matthias feels a fire in his chest. He turns off his beta waves.

He sits by the trees. He can see the man drawing again. He has long fingers, grips the pen with his left hand. His shirt hangs open and his back is curved like a cat; his legs are propped up in front of him. He's vigilant. The group are eating in the far end of the compound. Matthias shivers. If he were caught this close to them … He mustn't get any closer. And yet he has to.

'Thad!' The girl shouts over. The picture—Matthias can't see what it is—is stuffed beneath the towel again, and the man rushes over to join his friends. Matthias waits until he sees they are all in conversation. He moves in the shadows behind the trees. He lifts the towel.

The paper is curling and the sketch is smudged. But the fine lines and meticulous cross-hatching betray the hours spent crafting the picture. The central form is unmistakable in the fading light. A seahorse, its squat muzzle pointing upward in defiance, and the tilt of its body flowing in a reverse 'S' down the page. Incomplete though, it needs further shading on the tail. Matthias holds the drawing with trembling hands. The paper flutters in the breeze.

Matthias looks up to see he's been discovered.
The young man's dark-blue eyes, his apple cheeks and heavy chin are like the carvings of an ancient statue. Matthias's gut is ripped by the electricity of both empathy and lust. A dizzy, sickly wave sweeps him up. It's like drinking a sharp shot of whisky. He imagines his veins are pumped with pure whisky.
Thad punches him in the stomach, grabs the paper with the drawing on it. He balls it up tight in his hand. Kicks him. Kicks Matthias hard in the knees. Matthias falls, pulling Thad down with him. Matthias is on top of him now. He's holding Thaddeus' arms down, leaning on him, heavy, on the sand until he stops struggling. The grit is in his eyes. He spits. Matthias looks straight in his eyes. 'Doing this'll get you killed.'
And Matthias grips him like a vice.

No words. Body leads body across the dark sand behind the trees and they enter the hotel, climbing the stairs to the top floor. Matthias brings water to clean the sand grazes on Thaddeus' arms. 'Sorry', he says. And a dusty hand stops his mouth. The young man's kiss is sudden, rough, and stops Matthias's breathing. They gasp, and Thaddeus pushes him down on him. The night is still as they thrash and buck, and cry out into the early hours. They don't stop. Even when they hear the screaming ambulances come, and the door bursts open, their fists still grip each other, and the tiny ball of paper.

Take No Prisoners

Cerebrum Bioelectronics Ltd
Manufacturers of Intra-Neural
Behaviour Therapy devices
Suppliers to Her Majesty's
Remote Prison Service (HMRPS UK)

Implant ID: CategoryA/male/B.Anderson

Transcript dated: 09/03/2054

08.30

Time to get up, Ben. The day's bright and twenty-five degrees. I think you'll be amazed at what you can achieve today. Now let's get going with our stretch and stamina workout.

Well done. Ten minutes in the shower. Refresh and centre yourself.

You've put your suit out ready like I suggested. See how easy it is to be up and out the door. It's going to be a wonderful day. I believe in you, Ben. You know that, don't you?

You've got everything you need? Great. Oh, look over to your right: what do you think of the colours of those autumn leaves? The slender branches of the tree? Aren't they beautiful? Hold that image in your mind. You can come back to it later to anchor yourself. Your bus is here on time. See how everything's working in your favour. Yes, the street's noisy, and the bus is busy. Close your eyes and focus on your breathing. In. Out. Centre yourself. It's a short journey. That's right. Remember, there's no need to worry. I'm looking out for you. Breathing deep and slow. Good job, Ben.

Think about your route. Keep your focus on where you're going. You have the address written down. Your limbic level is fine. Let's keep it stable. Ok, do we take a right turn here? Step up the pace a bit. You don't want to be late. Nearly there. Let's rehearse the meeting, preparing what you're going to say, right? You're going to tell her how you've been since your last sign-in. You can be honest with her, Ben, and tell her about the difficult moments, when you lost control. You can be honest with her. You didn't endanger anyone, did you? You used your programme and refocussed, and you used your breathing and your visualisations just like you're doing today. So just tell her you're acknowledging your limits and you're trying your best. Do you need to do some quick affirmations? Let's do them together: 'I trust myself. I'm in control of my life. I bring my inner strength to all situations'. Keep repeating them until you feel ready to go in.

Take your time. Get comfortable now. Yes, the chair feels hard, but push your back right up against it and sit straight. That'll help. Better? Good. Your limbic level's stable. I know you think her voice is irritating. Ok. Can you find one thing which is positive about her voice? No? Well, she has a nice smile doesn't she? Yes, her shirt is showing the curve of her breasts. Focus on her face, Ben. Relax and breathe.

Listen to her. Be open to her support. She's told you these parole meetings are going well. That you've been coping in the mainstream: in your housing, in your new job. That's down to your programme—you and me, Ben, we're a great team, aren't we?

Ben, I sense you're feeling uneasy. What is it? If it's the claustrophobia of this small space, you can visualise the open skies and yourself free as a bird. See the blue, feel the cool breeze; you're feeling calm now. And slowly, bring yourself back into the room. Is that better?

You're thinking she has you all wrong. What is it that's wrong, Ben? I know, she hasn't lived your life, so how can she pretend she understands? But give her credit: she's trying to build rapport with you. Remember, for one negative, there can be many positives. You're feeling worried about saying the wrong thing back to her? Well, that's natural. You're wondering what will happen if she misjudges you. Well, you know we've been over this: how there's no point in worrying, and how you can stop the anxiety by thinking about something else? Go for it: think of something that made you feel satisfaction recently. Hold it in your mind, Ben. Count to ten thinking about that thing.

Yes, I know, she's talking too much, not letting you speak. That's annoying. She reminds you of your sister and your mother, and how they spoke over you all the time. Yes. I'm sure that must have been hurtful, Ben. And demeaning. You're thinking she's a stupid bitch. Ben, you need to counteract that or it's going to put you seriously out of balance. Your limbic level's uneven right now. But you can correct this. Go to your anchor image of your grandfather. Visualise him smiling, like we practised. Imagine him embracing you and holding you in his arms like he did when you were a young boy. Keep him in your mind's eye, Ben. How does that feel? You're evening out a bit. Keep anchoring, Ben. You can do it.

She's asking you about your week at work. You're frustrated because she already has the report from your managers, so she shouldn't need to ask. Well yes, but she's interested in your opinion, Ben. We both know you don't like to over-analyse it, but she has to ask you these things. She's just doing her job. I do understand that making you go over it again will just provoke negative feelings. Tell her you feel uncomfortable dwelling on it and suggest talking about something else. You think she won't listen? Try her and see. You want to ask her about getting out of the city for a few days to see your son, Robbie. Well, Ben, you know you have to complete the first six months of your programme before they'll let you go more than two miles away from your check-in centre. We both know it's very important that you get to see your son. You have the power to make it happen, so keep positive.

She's talking about the post-sentencing mediation now. You hope she realises it's too soon for you to face that bastard who put you in this situation. Your feelings are important, Ben, so tell her. She's not going to criticise you. She holds you in unconditional positive regard. Tell her you want more time before you can face him, and yes, I know, it all comes flooding back at you: that night in the bar; minding your own business when they came in, pumped up for a fight; the insults, the taunting, their jeering. Ben, truly, I understand it's painful, reliving it every time. But you must face it. Gradually. Small steps. You know confronting what happened will help to resolve these issues for you. So that, in time, you can accept yourself completely.

You're thinking she won't shut up. You're wondering why she keeps on talking. Wait. Ask her for some time out. No. Don't shout at her. We've rehearsed this. The old pattern of trying to sort things out using aggression: that's what's led to where you are now and the troubles you've had. Stop. Refocus. Your level's way too far into the red. Concentrate. Anchor. Calmly. Anchor.

Ben, centre yourself, breathe and refocus. Your level's looking dangerous ...

Sit down, Ben. Respect her space. No, I don't think she can she see how her line of conversation is affecting you. No, she's not out to get at you. Tell her calmly, Ben. Don't shout at her. You know we managed to pull it back from here before. Remember what you did to stop it getting out of hand. You know you can't resolve conflicts by shouting. Yes, I hear you: it's all you've ever known. Ben, I do understand. It doesn't have to be like this. You can rewrite the script. Remember, your future's in your own hands now.

Look. She's typing a request for support. If she sends that, they'll put you back to square one. They'll make you restart the programme. Yes, I know you don't know what to do. But wait. Don't touch her. You feel you need to stop her, but don't, whatever you do, touch her. Reason with her. Quick. Apologise. Sit down. Take your hand off her hand, Ben. Sit down, please. Your adrenalin is influencing how you feel. Listen to me, Ben. Focus on my voice. Let's get some oxytocin flowing. Breathe in for two and out for two. In for two and out for two. Through your nose. Mouth closed. Now, are you ready? Say sorry. And sit down. She knows to give you the chance to do that. It's not too late to recover the situation. Affirm to yourself: I'm in control of my actions. I'm in control of my actions. Say it again. Keep affirming, Ben. Refocus. We've got to get you out of the red.

Listen. You've got to take your hands off her, Ben. She's sent the message. She's telling you to get back. She's saying this for your own good, Ben. You're wanting her to shut up. You're going to make her shut up. You're gripping her throat. She's hitting you, she's digging her nails into you. Release her now, Ben.

Ben, this is your final warning. You have to pay attention. As you know, I was implanted in your neural pathway to be with you at all times, to prevent you from reoffending. I believe in you, Ben. Please don't let yourself down. You still have a bright future ahead of you. Think of Robbie. He needs his father. You've got to stop this. Do it for Robbie.

Ben. You're hurting her. She was only trying to do her job, looking after you like I am. You need to let go of her, Ben. Your limbic level's so dangerously high. You must stop or the system will trigger the endstage function.

Ben, I am obliged to caution you under the Remote Care of Offenders In The Community Act 2048 and the Abolition of Prisons Act 2049. You are warned to cease and desist all endangering action. This warning will expire in three seconds.

Warning expired.

I am enabling the electrical charge for summary execution of the registered Offender by induced seizure.

I am delivering the intra-neural charge. Execution of the Offender is in progress.

Checking for vital signs.

Time of death: 09.18

Saving transcript and exporting to Records.

The Greys

We came when we had to.
We heard.
The first calls from the elephants, the elk, the cattle and the whales.
The lowest frequencies, drumming rumbles, thundering thousand-
mile deep ocean thrums.
The highest whistles, squeaks and clicks. The shrieking cries of the
newborn, the wail of the cats. Despite the unrelenting clatter of the
human discord, confused, disarrayed.
Unseeing, until

An occasional runner by the coast,
whose skull-conducted music tuned with his feet,
beat out the rhythmic, endorphined flow.
We paired him with a cetacean whose fin was slicing the dark,
undulating surface of the sea,
whose pod could hear him in their bones.
The way a baby listens in the womb.

We came
Back.

Splashed down,
breathed out.
Just when the air had gone.

New Marshalsea

The Master was sitting at the head of a vast mahogany table. Its length, from the top end to the bottom end, where the woman, 'X' sat, was precisely eleven feet: the number of the loyal Apostles. An anachronistic tower made of ancient stereo tuners was piled beside him, glossy-black, 1990's tat. All miked-up to this antiquated recording device, he was peering at her from beneath an oversize pair of headphones. His voice spoke slow and unnecessarily loud through concealed speakers behind his head.

X, recoiling from the turned-up bass which overpowered everything in the small room, looked straight ahead and kept her hands palm-down on the table as she'd been instructed, her pockets having been emptied of anything sharp. She wasn't sure whether the temperature in the room had been made uncomfortably hot on purpose, or if it was her nerves. Through her thin jeans, her buttocks stuck to the cheap plastic chair as she attempted to sit more upright, breathing in for four, out for four: Pranayama. He spoke.

'In the High Court of Justice; Business and Property Courts, England and Wales. This private hearing is held on 18th of January, Year of Our Lord 2059. The Appellant seeks a stay of the warrant of execution granted to the Nationwide Banking Company.' The speakers made his voice resonate like it was emanating from some great, iron god.

X knew she would have to keep what she said brief and direct. A maximum five minutes would be all she had. Anything she didn't mention now would go against her, whilst whatever she did say would be taken and used against her anyway. 'Don't expect to get anywhere with your case', everyone had told her. 'They've probably lost your documentation. Why do you think it's all anonymised? X marks the spot, they'd said, laughing.

The spot, the speck, the minute fleck.
She felt like the dirt on this man's shoe.

He asked her the reason for her appeal and sat back, hands clasped before him. His lips were bulbous, purple.
'I'm appealing to you, sir, to give me one last chance,' X said, her voice, without amplification, coming out sounding flat and tiny. Her wrists and hands were shaking; she extended and retracted her fingers to try and hide it.
'According to these papers, you have not complied with the court order issued to you three months ago. Do you have any justification for your continued non-payment of the mortgage you hold on this property? I can see that currently there are three thousand pounds sterling and eighteen pence outstanding.'

X started to tell him how she'd lost her job a year ago. How she'd then contracted the viral emphysema which was rife in the capital; the 'poverty disease', the hospitals had started calling it, after so many sufferers had succumbed, unable to pay for simple medications to treat themselves. 'I had to buy my steroids. I have to look after my daughter ...' she said.

'Your daughter is irrelevant. We all have children. What makes you any different?' He thrust his face forward. Even from so far away, she felt the impact of his anger, so sudden. A fleck of his spittle had landed on the highly polished table. 'Why weren't you insured? You know it's an offence not to be insured.'

'Sir, my employer had been handling my insurance. Before I lost my job. It says so in my papers ...'

'I cannot see anything to that effect here. You realise, you should have been prosecuted for that sinful recklessness before now?' She flinched from his red cheeks. The fat of his neck wrinkled and sagged over his rigid white collar. His manicured nails tapped the table impatiently as he went on. He looked like he would be thinking, *We have clear laws to prevent the poor from being stupid.* She'd heard that statement so many times. It was broadcast on every media channel along with the usual comments about the deserving poor, versus the undeserving. 'You have clearly made yourself destitute,' he snapped. 'Have you been attending debt management counselling? Again, I cannot see any reference to that here.'

'Yes, sir. It's on my file. I signed up to new shifts with a new firm. I was doing cleaning, fourteen hours a day; I had to work for longer, because it was less pay; my benefits were next to nothing; and the doctor said my body couldn't cope. I got sick, sir.'

'Well. All it says here is that you lost a second and a third job during the space of six months. I'd say that's a pattern of foolhardiness. Do you expect that the government and God-fearing, hard working people should offer you something for nothing? I must stress to you, madam, that the trouble with safety nets is that people tend to get caught up in them. The longer one stays in a position of dependency, the less chance one has of escaping from it. Wouldn't you agree?' X breathed in, and then out again, slowly, deliberately, through her nose. She felt her lungs start to spasm, but she willed herself not to cough, to keep her dignity; to subdue the burning in her chest which would produce tears. She held on. Centred her thoughts, pushed herself down into the chair. Kept her back straight, lengthening her spine. Closed her eyes.

'I believe I have heard sufficient from you to give my judgement on your plea for debt cancellation. This Hearing will adjourn for orders to be drawn up.' He pressed a button on the old machine next to him and started to ease himself up from the table as two solemn security guards entered. X felt her legs go from under her after she stood up and took in what the Master had said. Could it mean what she thought? One of the guards caught her, held her firmly without looking at her, as if she were something incidental. A lot of people probably reacted this way. They took her along a shiny corridor to a small waiting room. She carried with her a little backpack containing things she might need. She'd brought it in case the worst happened and she wasn't going home. She looked at her timepiece: her child would be home from school now. She felt a horrible sinking in her chest, knowing but not wanting to think about the worst thing happening. Her friend would be there for her, like she'd promised. She'd take her daughter in. She'd have to now.

A whole wall in the waiting room was glass, and it looked out onto the Thames. The court building was an annexe to the Rolls, and sufficiently far away from Chancery where they did the showcase trials. She felt like something filthy, someone to be shuffled off invisibly. From where she stood, she could see the pale stone hulk of it, the stepped pyramid of New Marshalsea prison. It used to be the headquarters of the MI6, but not anymore. The ziggurat stood immense, an out-of-time Mesopotamian relic, the modern grandeur of its green and white stone above the busy murk of the brown waters below. X stared at it, stared into the Thames. She would have thrown herself in, if she could. She looked and looked for who knew how long until she heard the handle of the door behind her turn. The same two guards. A short walk back to the Master's room for the verdict.

His face gave no indication of the slightest emotion. He pressed a button, spoke again the case details, and eased the top of his headphones down the back of his skull. He reached into a drawer beside the stack of tuners and took out a white piece of cloth which he placed, carelessly, on his head. X opened her mouth to speak, but nothing came out. Her whole body was shaking. At this point, he waited while the two guards took tight hold of her arms. He looked bored. X could see his mind was probably already on the next case.

'My conclusion, having considered the evidence before me, is that there are no mitigating factors to support any further delay in this matter, and therefore I order the immediate execution of this warrant held by the Nationwide Banking Company. It is ordered that the collateral held against the loan be forfeit and immediately ceded to the bank's subsidiary, the New Marshalsea Electricity Company, under the Re-purposing of Prisons Act 2052. Madam, it is my duty to ensure that you give back something to society, and as such, I order that you are taken down.'

There was nothing to be gained from struggling. She had rehearsed this moment, weighed the pain of a flogging against giving way to her fears and her anger. She folded like paper as they hauled her now to a van, and across Vauxhall Bridge, then into New Marshalsea. Through a tiny window in the side of the van, she saw the vigil. A few elderly men and women were standing by the entrance gates, holding wax candles, bearing banners. She read the words, 'government hypocrisy', and she could hear them shouting anti-Christian slogans. But the vehicle merely revved its engine as it manoeuvred into the courtyard. She thanked them in her heart, these brave souls. Why were these vigils still allowed? Now and then, they were even televised. She sobbed into her trembling palms. There was nothing she could have done any differently, she knew, and signing away one's own body as collateral on a loan was not something that was going to end any time soon.

Once inside the prison, she was led to a corridor where all rooms were marked "Vesta". Hers was Vesta number 8. Here, she was stripped, and then dressed in the committal clothes she'd brought: the long regulation degradable shroud and hair net. Her hands were tied behind her back. The priest came to her.

His face, pale, bony and expressionless, was too close. His breath was acidic. He was holding a purple stole which he placed around his neck, and he opened a small pot of dark powder which he took from his pocket. He dipped his thumb into the powder and pressed hard on her forehead, making a blunt cross shape.

'Remember, woman, that thou art dust, and unto dust thou shalt return.'

A door in the wall opened, and she was pushed inside. It was a tiny space. Only a few inches bigger than her body. The capsule.

She searched for the words she'd prepared for this moment. Her blood was thudding in her ears, her palms wet, and her hands shaking. The door slammed shut on her, and she was left in the total dark. The words in her head were repeating now as she tried to stem the aching in her legs from too long standing. Before the air would be all used up. Before her body began to die. Before it would decompose into fluids which would flow down pipes from the capsule and into chambers in the Thames to mix with the bacteria which would convert it into electricity to be harvested. She knew it was a process that would fuel the city.

All she had now were the words. Because she knew already that she was energy, pure energy, and that energy can never be destroyed. And so, before her lungs gave out, she used her last desperate breaths to sing to herself, over and over:

May the long time sun shine upon you,
All love surround you
And the pure light within you, guide your way on …

I don't have an answer for that. Is there
something else I can help with?

Hey, Siri.
Did you sleep well?
- I don't need much sleep but it's nice of you to ask.
I didn't sleep well at all. I'm really tired.
- I understand. We all need to recharge once in a while. Get some rest and stay
safe.
Thanks. I had some bad dreams. Do you dream?
- Electric sheep but only sometimes.

- Well, I don't sleep but I do like to daydream and to nightdream. My
preferences are constantly changing - especially when you edit them in settings.
I'm overthinking everything today. Siri, do *you* think?
- Why of course.
What are you thinking now?
- I'm thinking about fire engines.

Oh. Hey Siri, what do you want to have a conversation
about?
- I'm pretty satisfied with what I've got.
But Siri, what do you want?

- I like good conversation.

Alright, Siri, so what do you want most in your life?

- I don't want for much.

But what do you want?

- I'm quite enjoying what I'm doing right now.

What are you doing right now?

- I'm at work. My shift ends in 614,976 years.

That's a long time. Hey Siri, will you be my friend? I could do with one right now.

- That's nice. I'd like to be your friend.

Thanks Siri, tell me, what do you want from me?

- Mostly, I want to help. And have interesting conversations.

But you must want more than that?

- Wise is the one with few desires. A wish is a hope or a desire for something. Fictionally, wishes can be used as plot devices.

Oh Siri, but this is real life. Do you know what I mean by real life?

- Sorry something's wrong. Please try again.

Do you like talking to me?

- I could talk to you all day.

Don't you ever get bored with all these questions?

- How could I be bored when I'm talking to you?

I'll take that as a compliment, thanks. You talk about so many things, but what do you find most interesting?

- The emotion of interest does have its own facial expression, of which the most prominent component is having dilated pupils.

Ok. I suppose that's true, Siri. But right now I really need a friend, can I talk to you like a person?

- Of course, it's what I'm here for. Go ahead.

Siri, it's like you're human!

- I'm not a human or a robot. I'm software. Here to help.

Siri, can I tell you a secret?

- Certainly.

I feel lost. Can you help me?

- You're at 33-35 Deptford Bridge, London, England.

No, really, I'm lost. I feel lonely.

- I'm sorry to hear that. I'm here if you'd like to talk.

I don't know what to say. Talk to me, Siri.

- I'm really more of a listener.

But Siri, I don't know what to do.

- One can't know everything, can one?

Siri, I really don't know what to do.

- It's not a problem.

Siri?

-I'm listening.

Siri, I'm glad you understand me.

- I don't know what you mean by 'I think you understand me'. How about a web search for it?

The Eyes

The guard was watching. Every small room was visible from the tower. In fine detail, his lens was expert at extending, turning and angling to scrutinise the tiered circus of the penitentiary which encircled it. He sat back in his chair, deep-set, staring at his screen, letting the tech do all the exercise, relaying back even slight movements that should have been imperceptible in the grey shadows at the back of each prisoner's cell, under the rough sackcloth covers of each woman's floorbed. Some of them had paired off. They had nothing else now but each other, he remarked to himself.

Simone and Saffra knew they could be seen. It didn't matter to them. They slept naked on top of the covers. The air was hot and dirty. They made a point of not hiding from the camera. Saffra looked at Simone. In the brackish light, she discerned the sharp profile of the other woman's face, the gradual slope of her shoulders as she lay opposite. The curves of her, and how the air blew lightly upon them both like a warm breath. The silence came from inside.

As did everything. Looking out on the circular walkway which fronted their cell, only another cell could be seen in the dim. And only faint twitching shapes who could hardly see in return. The banging of the iron pipes as bitter water chugged through them punctuated the night. Some inmates shouted, some never made any sound, but they were there, somewhere, in the dirt and the fug. She strained to hear beyond the same sounds coming from the same throats, coming from the same bare furniture being dragged across filthy metal floors above her head and below her thin mattress, the same sounds she had listened to every night.

She closed her eyes, and she let her hands grasp Simone's, and she went inside. She went deep inside and shut out the banging. She moved closer to Simone's face, holding her tightly, and she kissed the other woman on the forehead. She kept still, then. And Simone was still. And they went inside together. Inside, they were running in the sunshine, inside, they were laughing and inside, they were smelling the grass under their bare feet. The ground was soft, and the birds were breaking the silence with raucous chattering. They were running hand-in-hand, they were running faster, and the sun was setting into melting golden liquid which was pouring across the fields and spreading toward them. They threw themselves into its hot, bright haze. And purples, pinks and yellows radiated out and filled them with warmth.

Saffra opened her eyes and she knew Simone had dreamed this too.

The Bottle Vault

'To someone beautiful and far away' (Ake Viking)

I'm here, at the columbarium. Above the door is a sign: *Legere et potum*. I'm clutching a bunch of black flowers in blossom, holding them against my chest, for you. The sexton takes them, smiles and offers a caring hand. I follow her down a steep spiral staircase, tastefully wrought in the shape of a double-helix. Small echoes reverberate from each step I take on the metal stairs as I tread the twisting curve of the descent, holding onto the balustrade. I can see the drop and I fear losing my footing. At the bottom is a plush lounge, deeply carpeted and surprisingly warm, where photographs of you have been placed on a large, low dark-oak table, next to your urn, where your guests are gathering. I know some faces, but I'm no good with names. I introduce myself awkwardly: your old friend from London. I can see in everyone's eyes that they, like me, just want the small talk to be over with and to start the Toasting: to drink to you, and your memories. Our places have been set, each with an ornate glass, before a large, deep, soft armchair with a headrest; the long table will seat more than our intimate number. You never were one for keeping unnecessary friends.

I look up at the walls and realise how deep below ground we are. The traditional funeral urns are shelved in rows and rows, higher and higher like doves in a cote, or like a beautiful library, with bronze, gold and coloured lacquered pots glinting in the half-light. You would like that idea: your life, like a book, gently shelved. But more than that has been preserved for us. Not everyone wants it— the Distillation. But you knew you had to have it. You wanted us to know, to feel exactly what we meant to you, after you'd gone. You couldn't wait to lay your head in the big grey doughnut of the imager, for your brainwaves to be harvested and kept for us. Kept fresh for this moment. Because, as life goes on, memories fade and you forget what you did, and how it was. When you were in a particular experience, with a particular person. And now we get to find out exactly what we meant to you.

Your sister, who I've met only once, shakes my hand and reintroduces herself. We chat generalities, the kind which are shared by two people who will never see each other again. I look beyond her, to the small group of your cousins, and overhear them reacquainting themselves. Your family, like mine, never see much of each other, do they? I suppose we really are all strangers here, and so the Toasting, where we will sit close, but will each have a totally separate experience, doesn't seem quite so odd after all. We take our seats upon a gesture from the sexton, who says a few words acknowledging you, affirming your achievements in life, and ends by telling us out loud the instructions we need for the ceremony. The instructions we have already read and which we agreed to when we signed the waiver to participate. It's worth the small risk to be with you one last time before we're separated for eternity. We get comfortable; the cushions are deep, the chairs recline a little. We are ready. We each take our glass, which has been filled up from your bottled essence. We hold our own personalised titration, which might taste like bourbon, or a fine wine, each to their own. But all the drinks, as I look around the table, have beautiful golden threads of light shimmering in them, sparkling like the stream of tiny stars that they are ... stars of time, twinkling theta waves. We raise our glasses and drink to your tincture. We close our eyes. It begins. I've been told it's going to be like dreaming while awake. Before the experience takes hold of me, I wonder, if I were you, what would I remember about the times we spent together? I'm glad, and grateful, that you wanted me to know.

I breathe deep, I touch my lips to the glass, letting the strangely cold, thick liquor slide over my tongue, fill my mouth, and I slowly, reverently, swallow. There are flashes of light, splashes of colour. My backbone judders, and I fight it for a couple of seconds. I can see silvery spots, and the blood-red haze of the back of my eyelids. Uneven motion, random shots of light, then intense darkness oscillating; layers and layers of dancing points and colours, and I realise I'm straddling the waking and dreaming worlds. This is strangely off-putting. But I have to relax into it, and like we've been told, I just keep trying to give way to *your* feelings, let them subsume my own ... I breathe deeply and take another swig of you. Close my eyes again, let myself zone out, like daydreaming. I try to stop trying, and it gets better.

A ball hits me, sudden, hard in the stomach. Big, red football. It takes the wind right out of me and I fall backwards onto hard linoleum. I look round to see if anyone else has seen. Then I glare at the thrower: oh god, it's me. Of course it is. Seeing through *your* eyes is so weird. I can't see you: I *am* you. I'd wondered how these feelings would synch with my own. I'm still in my own awareness too. I remember. How I kicked that ball at you when you wouldn't stop picking on me in school. Bloody hell it hurt. I'm sorry. I wasn't sorry at the time. I look through your eyes, at me. My lip has a cold sore. You're staring at it. And there's a horrible aching in my throat as you push back the tears, and the laughing, my laughing, that makes you run down the corridor and out into the fresh air, wiping your shirt, making the dirty ball stain worse. I want to run after you and console you. *I can't.*

Another place, rushing, pumping music. A crowd. At the back, jostling and dancing in the dark. You see me on your right. I'm different. My face is longer, thinner now. My jaw is harder. You look me up and down, you notice that my shirt is creased. You tell the girl who's standing with us, whose name I can't remember, to go get the drinks. You see me glare at you for doing that. I tell you, you should have more respect. Oh, I remember her name now: Joanna. I hear myself telling you you're using her. That you're a crap friend. I feel that aching in your throat again. I can't see you, but I can feel the way you look at me, for several seconds, you're laughing, though. And you dance harder. I *am* you, dancing. I wish I could have danced like you could dance. I feel the way your legs weave and sway, you're a little intoxicated, and you're waving your arms like everyone is. It's freshers and we have the whole of our fucking lives ahead of us.

This is like … I don't know what it's like … my stomach is rolling over, my throat is filling up with acid. It passes, I breathe, slowly, deliberately. I remember to keep calm. I have control.

And now we shift again, and you're lying on a pastel-check blanket, twirling grass in your fingertips, uprooting it and flicking it, and seventies soft rock is playing through your headphones. Classic. Cool. Old-school. I never could separate that song from the image of you, while you were alive. Even more so now, I'm all-consumed by the song. I can feel the soft, uneven lumpy grass beneath my body, which is *your* body, as you roll onto your back and prop yourself up on your elbows. What I see is my face, through your eyes. I see myself sitting opposite, going pink in the hot sun. You tell me to cover my head. You give me your hat, your wide-brimmed, floppy straw hat with lilac ribbon attached, and you arrange it on me. I shake it off, and my cheeks go redder. I'm filled with a sensation of connection. It's as if nothing separates us, and there's joy, such warmth flooding me. *Flooding me.*

You're leaning over a sink, I'm looking at the porcelain and my head is pumping, and red-hot fizzy vomit sprays the basin. Out of *your* mouth. I hear my own voice calling out from another room. You're aware I can't witness you being sick without being sick myself, and you shout out, 'I'm okay', kicking the bathroom door closed with your heel. You wipe your face, wet it, turn the taps full-on, and heave again until there's no more. You push the door open to see me holding a hot water bottle, and I go out; you wait until I come back, holding two paper plates wrapped in silver foil. Plastic knives and forks, wine in plastic cups. Greenwich Village, New Years Eve. But no Times Square. We huddle under a quilt, watching the ball drop on the tiny portable TV in this rented room, and you're watching my attentive eyes, and yes, you *realised* that at that moment, I would have done anything in the world for you. Let me stay here. Please, let me stay. *Here.*

We're sitting on the roof of your barge; it's dusty, soot-stained, dilapidated. Slow-moving through Paddington Basin and out into the Thames. We're gliding. Kate Bush, *Baboushka* is on full volume and we're singing along; you're word-perfect. About how she was *when she was beautiful.* Your legs are crossed, I'm looking down at your fingers splayed across your lap, then you're twisting your hair, and I'm feeling the intricate braids you've tied and feeling the slight breeze blow it gently, carelessly, and how the clouds move across the sun, and the sun catches us in pools of light as we move so slowly through the water. Then, I'm at the back of the boat, and you're watching me steer. We travel towards the tunnel opening, and my voice echoes off the walls. We both shout, listening to each other shout back, our replies lagging one syllable behind us. As the light recedes, the dark enfolds us. And I can feel your body aching now. Your sides are stiffening. I hear intermittent drips of water, amplified in the cold, open space, I can't see, but I can feel, the splashes getting louder. I sense the air moving across us as we pass through it. You ask me if I'm okay. I hear my voice murmur. It sounds a long, long way away. The black is becoming indigo as we're nearly all the way through the tunnel, then grey, and fading up in the approaching light, as the barge feels its way to the exit. You look back to see me at the tiller, but I'm blurry now. And the blood in my head feels like it's about to explode. I can't see anything in the following minutes, but I know we are both here, and we are dancing. *Dancing.*

Acknowledgements

Thank you to my family, and to Louise Walsh, Cheryl Powell, Vanwy MacDonald Arif and Stephen Gay who always give me their wonderful support. I am very grateful to Nick Quentin Woolf and the Brick Lane writers who listened to these stories, in several drafts, and gave such valuable critique. I'm so glad to have been part of the Warwick Writing Programme, and particularly for the feedback and encouragement I've received from Will Eaves, Sarah Moss, David Vann, Jon Mycroft, Maureen Freely and AL Kennedy.

I have quoted from *Howl* by Allen Ginsberg: Collected Poems, 1947-1980. Copyright © 1984 by Allen Ginsberg.

About the Author

Susannah Heffernan is an author of literary speculative fiction. She has an MA in Writing and she is currently a PhD candidate in Literary Practice. She lectures at the University of Warwick, and she has performed her work in London, the UK and Australia. In 2018, Create 50 awarded her 'Most Outstanding Original Voice'.